W9-BSF-761

Dedicated to my amazing husband Tom and my wonderful son Caden.
Thank you for fully supporting me on this journey.

Printed in the United States of America

ISBN 978-0-9896700-1-2

First Edition

The text for this book is set in Veggieburger.
The illustrations for this book are rendered in acrylic paint.

 Sleepy Sheep Publishing, LLC

Drumsticks

Written & Illustrated by
Dawn Hubbell

Chicken couldn't wait to get started making her vegetable soup.
It always got such rave reviews down at the chicken coop.
But on her way to the kitchen she noticed something strange.
Cow and Pig were whispering in a secretive exchange.

Being a nosy kind of chicken,
she leaned in so she could hear.

She couldn't make everything out,
but one thing she heard quite clear.

Cow said, "Let's make Chicken drum sticks and then we'll have a feast!"

She gasped

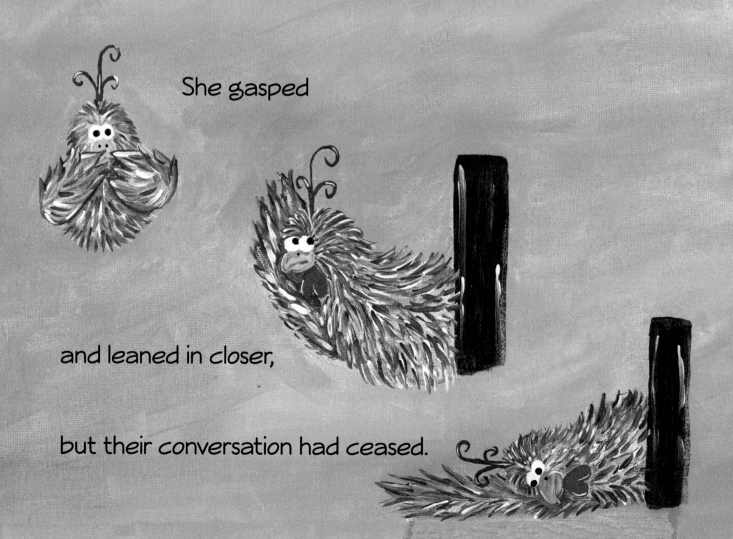

and leaned in closer,

but their conversation had ceased.

Chicken couldn't believe what she'd heard and she got a dreadful hunch.

Was it even possible that she was to become their lunch?

She fussed and fretted for awhile and
decided to go take a look.

She intended to find out exactly
what her friends were going to cook.

In the kitchen she saw her friend
Goat reaching for a pot.

As she watched him rummage around
her throat tied in a knot.

"I can't wait to make Chicken drum sticks!"
Goat said with a smile.

Chicken swallowed the lump in her throat
as he threw the pots in a pile.

Next she hid and watched
as Pig gathered up some wood.

"These logs will make
fine drum sticks,
oh that sounds so good!"

Was Pig planning on making a fire to baste and cook her in?
As she wiped her sweating brow her head began to spin.

She had to run, she had to hide, she had to get away.
For who knew what would happen if she decided to stay.

After hiding for a bit, she heard them coming closer.

Why couldn't they just buy their lunch from the local grocer?

Alas, she wasn't very successful
at hiding from her friends.

They found her quite quickly and
she sensed . . .this is how it ends!

Please, oh please, she thought,
I don't want to be their meal.

As they escorted her away
she let out a little squeal.

On to the kitchen they strolled, marching in a straight line.
This is it she thought, on drumsticks they will dine.

When they went inside,
her friends all yelled out a big, "SURPRISE!"
At the same time Chicken shouted,

"Please, I want to keep my thighs!"

Seeing her friends' confused faces, she looked from left to right.
Sitting there in the corner was such a wonderful sight.

Three pots made up a set of drums
that sat against a wall.

And a pair of *wooden* drum sticks meant,
she wouldn't be lunch after all!

Goat had collected several pots
to make her a set of drums.

He hadn't intended after all to
cook her with some crumbs!

And the logs that Pig had
very carefully selected,

were made into drum sticks, not
the fire that she expected.

Then she spotted a table holding the feast that they had planned.
With fresh vegetables, salads, and breads, it all looked so grand!
And she noticed with such relief and a joyful flutter in her heart,
that the feast was vegetarian, so no one had lost their parts!

"We want you to join our barnyard band,"
Sheep said with a smile.

"You're the best drummer around and we
really like your style."

Chicken was so happy,
it was all a silly mistake!

She would not be going
after all, into the oven to bake!

She explained what she had thought was going to be her fate.
Pig mused,"I'd rather have drum sticks in our band than
sitting on my plate!"

They all wholeheartedly agreed that what Pig had said was true.
Because having friends **to** lunch and not **for** lunch is a really nice
thing to do.

Chicken decided to join the band and with her new drum sticks they sounded great.

And when they had finished playing a few songs they all sat down and ate.

Chicken even made her famous vegetable soup, which they all slurped with delight.

And she decided that at this meal, more than any other, she would savor every bite.

About the Author:

Dawn Hubbell was born and
raised in the rural town of
Pownal, Vermont. Her love for
animals and nature started at a young age, as well
as her love for writing and creating art. Upon graduating
from college she worked for seven years in the animal
care field and volunteered at a farm animal sanctuary.
She now resides in New York with her husband and
their son and three furry adopted family members.
She hopes to write children's books that foster
compassion towards animals and harmony with nature.

Made in the USA
Middletown, DE
17 March 2015